ENCHANTED PONY ACADEMY

Dreams That Sparkle

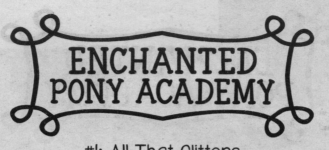

ENCHANTED PONY ACADEMY

ENCHANTED PONY ACADEMY

Dreams That Sparkle

✳ Lisa Ann Scott ✳

✳ illustrated by Heather Burns ✳

SCHOLASTIC INC.

Text copyright © 2017 by Lisa Ann Scott

Illustrations by Heather Burns, © 2017 Scholastic Inc.

ISBN 978-0-545-90897-9

10 9 8 7 6 5 4 3 2 1   17 18 19 20 21

Printed in the U.S.A.

First printing 2017

Book design by Yaffa Jaskoll

To my editors,
Abby and Amanda, for making
the Glitter Ponies extra sparkly
and fabulous!

CHAPTER 1

Belissima took a deep breath and looked around her stall in the Earth barn. She couldn't believe that selection week was actually here! In just a few days, she'd be leaving Enchanted Pony Academy. She *hoped* she'd be leaving—this week the royal children were coming to the Academy to pick a graduating pony as their royal pet. If Belissima was chosen, she'd move to a new kingdom and use her magic to help rule!

For now, she was more nervous than excited. So many emotions were swirling inside of her: excitement, fear, sadness, and glee. She'd never felt this way before, not even the day she first climbed the rainbow stairs to join the academy two years ago.

"How are you going to style your mane? It's such a beautiful color," Skydancer asked, rustling her wings just outside Belissima's stall door.

Belissima flicked her tail. "I'm not doing anything special."

Rose poked her nose in. "Why not?"

"Because she doesn't have to do anything to look amazing. She's already so pretty," Razzle said, joining the group. "Belissima, you're going to be First Pony, I'm sure of it."

"Oh, I don't know about that," Belissima said.

"Of course you're going to be chosen first. You're so gorgeous that everyone will want you for a pet," Razzle said.

Belissima stomped her hoof. "That's not the only reason for children to select their royal pony."

Skydancer nodded. "Right, our Glitter Gifts are important, too." Skydancer was a first-year pegapony who could talk to any other winged creature. It was an amazing and useful gift. She'd been able to communicate with the two young dragons that had landed near their school. Without Skydancer's Glitter Gift, no one would have known they were looking for help, not trouble.

Belissima frowned. Her Glitter Gift wasn't very exciting. Her coat could change color and sparkle. Big deal. That had placed her in the pageantry study group. She really loved her healing classes and would've preferred that group instead, but a color-changing coat had nothing to do with healing. So she'd spent the last two years perfecting different gaits and fancy moves, like riding a figure-eight and walking on her hind legs. She'd worked her hardest in her classes, but pageantry skills weren't her true passion.

Daisy galloped into the stables with a tray levitated by her side. "Happy selection week! We made you a treat! It just came out of the oven. It's posy pie!"

"Oh, thank you," said Belissima. It was tradition for the first-year students to present gifts to the graduating ponies during selection week. Some ponies put together performances or wrote songs and poems. Belissima thought it was a lovely gesture.

"I found the *Magic Treats and Eats Cookbook* in the library," Daisy said proudly.

"It's filled with surprise recipes. All the first-year ponies from Earth barn worked on the pie together. Take a taste and see what happens." Daisy giggled and tried to hide her smile.

"Is this a trick?" Belissima asked.

"A good one," Rose said. "You're going to love it!"

Belissima took a small bite of the fruity pie. As soon as her lips touched the treat, a cloud of flower petals fluttered in the air all around her. "Oh, how wonderful!"

"And your breath will smell like flowers for a while!" Daisy said.

Belissima laughed, and indeed, she smelled a lovely floral scent.

"There are so many interesting recipes," Daisy said. "The ponies in Water barn made cloud candy. It's cotton candy that floats!"

Razzle frowned. "Stone wanted to make the *atchoo* cookies. The recipe said it would make a pony sneeze for hours!"

"He's nothing but a jokester," said

Skydancer, frowning. "Good thing we found the cookbook first."

"There were other horrible recipes that seemed like pranks, instead of wonderful surprises," Daisy said. "I even saw one that gives you moldy green spots all over your coat!"

"Oh my!" Belissima said.

"Don't worry, we hid the cookbook in the library where Stone will never find it," Razzle said.

Skydancer giggled. "Behind *The Complete History of the Hundred Kingdoms*. Have you seen the size of that book? He'll never look there."

All the ponies laughed with her.

Electra bounded into the barn with several flower garlands draped over her neck. "Happy selection week! The ponies in Sky barn made one for each of the ponies in the selection ceremony. I saved the prettiest one for you, Belissima, since you're the prettiest pony."

Belissima forced a smile. No one ever mentioned she had the top grades in her class, or that she was a leader who always tried to be patient and pleasant with all the ponies at school. The only thing anyone ever said about Belissima was that she was pretty. Or beautiful. Or gorgeous. She really hoped whichever child chose her could see that she was so much more than her looks.

The prince or princess who would be her perfect match would love to explore fields of flowers and chase butterflies until they fluttered off into the sky. They'd splash through creeks and frolic under waterfalls. Together, they'd creep through spooky forests and collect wild herbs to make healing potions. They'd both get so muddy, no one would be able to tell what shade of purple Belissima was.

But her perfect match would *not* spend time brushing her mane or decorating her hooves. They would not try countless head-dresses and accessories on her. They would not waste their time primping and preening. A mirror would not be needed in her stable.

Electra levitated the garland around Belissima's neck.

"Thank you, Electra," she said. "This must have taken a lot of work to create."

"It did. I conjured up a spell to help me weave the flowers."

"Excellent! Keep working hard and your magic will continue to grow," Belissima said.

Electra's horn and hooves suddenly glowed. It was a wonderful Glitter Gift.

"We better go get our seats before the ceremony starts," Skydancer said. "We'll be cheering for you. Just think, in a few days, you'll be leaving the academy with your royal child! I can't wait to meet your perfect match."

Belissima felt panicked realizing how much she'd miss these friends she'd come to love so much. The child who chose her just *had* to be her perfect match. Otherwise, they'd both be so very unhappy.

She raised her chin, determined to put her best hoof forward during selection week. She had to be sure the children could see beyond her pretty coat and fancy mane.

CHAPTER 2

The stadium was filled with royal families waiting for the first event of the week to begin: the formal introduction. Many of the Glitter Ponies' families had made the trip, too. Belissima scanned the crowd for her mother. The two of them had always been so close, and it had been difficult to leave her behind to attend the academy. Her father had died when Belissima was just a young filly, and her mother had no other children.

Belissima grinned when she spotted her in the stands, and her mother bobbed her head in greeting. Belissima had worked very hard these past two years to make her mother proud. To make up for leaving her. It was too bad she didn't have something more impressive than a few pageantry tricks to show off, Belissima thought. She wished again that she were a healer, the type of pony who could've saved her father when he got sick.

Trumpets sounded, and the ponies lined up in alphabetical order. That meant Belissima would be one of the first ones introduced by Headmaster Elegius and Headmistress Valincia. She had to do her very best. Her mother would be so disappointed if she wasn't chosen this week.

Belissima gazed at the thrones at the end of the arena, recognizing many of the children who would be selecting ponies this week. She'd met most of them during their riding lessons over the past two years, but as she watched their excited faces now, she realized she hadn't felt a special spark with any of them. The girls had always gushed over her looks, but she'd never made a real connection with them.

This is going to be harder than I thought! She took another deep breath, trying not to panic. *But my perfect match will see me for who I really am. They have to.*

The royal children looked very grown-up in their regal attire. Crowns glittered in the sun, and capes rustled in the light breeze. Nervous chatter filled the air. They had journeyed from faraway lands and traveled up and over the rainbow to the hidden school just for this occasion.

Headmaster Elegius and Headmistress Valincia approached the podium and the crowd hushed.

"Glitter Pony families, ladies and gentlemen from the hundred kingdoms, welcome to our annual spring selection ceremony," the headmaster said. "Our ponies have been training hard, working on their magical skills in order to be worthy assistants to help these royal children rule

their lands. We are so very pleased to introduce the eighteen ponies in this graduation class!"

That was the ponies' cue to gallop around the stadium together. Andover and Alia were ahead of Belissima and she charged behind them.

A burst of applause filled the stadium as the ponies entered the arena. The air shimmered as their sparkly hooves left clouds of glitter behind them.

Belissima felt a surge of excitement while trotting in front of the hundreds of spectators. After dreaming about it for so long, selection week was finally here. Maybe she'd been worried about nothing.

She galloped back to their starting position and waited for the headmistress to call her to the small stage in front of the children. It reminded her of when she'd first entered the academy and all the new ponies had to show off their Glitter Gifts. She'd been so embarrassed that she could only turn her coat a different color, but the children had been thrilled. Thankfully, she'd learned much more magic than that during her time at school.

Today was just a quick introduction, showing off each pony's Glitter Gift again and a short presentation in their study concentration. Then over the next three days, the ponies from each study group would perform more advanced demonstrations of their work. On the fourth day, the children would make their selection. The fifth and final day would end with the good-bye ceremony. Belissima wondered if all the other ponies were as nervous as she was.

Alia tossed her mane as she ran back from the stage, and whispered, "Good luck!" to Belissima.

Now the headmistress was calling her name. "Please give a warm welcome to Belissima!"

Belissima trotted toward the stage showing off her cantering that she'd worked so hard to perfect.

"Belissima has focused her studies on pageantry," the headmistress said. "But she is also the top pony in her class for grades, and she was lead pony of Earth barn, providing guidance to her fellow ponies."

Belissima proudly stepped up onto the platform in front of the children. A few of the boys looked bored, but the girls were smiling and waving at her.

"Hi, Belissima!" called one girl who had ridden her several times. "I hope I can choose you. No one in the hundred kingdoms will have a prettier pet!"

"Better hope your name is drawn first in the selection lottery. She's definitely going to be the first pony picked," said the boy next to her.

"I want to pick her!" said another girl.

"And now for Belissima's Glitter Gift," the headmistress announced, interrupting the children's chatter.

Belissima closed her eyes and imagined her coat changing color. Some ponies had to work much harder to conjure up their Glitter Gift, but by now, she could just think of it to make it happen. Secretly, she thought there must not be much magic needed to make such a simple gift appear.

The crowd cheered and she knew her coat must have changed.

She opened her eyes and spotted a beautiful princess seated at the back of the group. The girl tipped up her chin, surveying Belissima. She'd only ridden with Belissima once before, and she certainly hadn't felt a spark with that girl, not the way a pony is supposed to when they find their perfect match in a royal child. In fact, they hadn't even talked very much during their time together.

But now the girl raised an eyebrow,

seeming very interested in Belissima. The princess was breathtakingly beautiful with long, curly black hair and big, dark eyes. She wore the fanciest dress of all the girls. Gems and pearls were tucked in among her curls, and her crown was the biggest and most elaborate of all the children's. Each one of her nails had an intricate design painted on.

It must have taken her hours to get ready for this ceremony.

Belissima flared her nostrils, imagining the endless days this princess would certainly spend curling her mane and braiding her tail with strands of silk and beads. She'd probably douse her with perfume and brush her coat for hours. Life would be filled with boring parades and parties. They probably would never venture outside for fear of getting dirty. It would be no fun at all being her pet.

Please don't pick me, thought Belissima as she trotted backstage. *Anyone but her!*

CHAPTER 3

When the official introductions were complete, the graduating ponies returned to the arena so the royal children could spend time with them. A tall prince ran right up to Ranger. They'd spent many hours riding together during lessons, and it appeared they were a perfect match.

A group of girls circled Belissima, debating which shade of purple her coat was. "It's violet," said one girl.

"No, I'd call it periwinkle!" argued her friend.

"Amethyst?" suggested another.

Belissima couldn't focus on what they were saying. She was too busy watching the perfect princess inspect her from the edge of the crowd.

Crossing her arms, the girl looked Belissima up and down. She was probably trying to decide what kind of saddle blanket to have custom-made for her. No doubt, she'd have a different one for each day of the week.

After spending a few more moments staring at Belissima, the girl turned and left the stadium. She didn't visit any of the other ponies. Had she already decided to choose Belissima?

"I wonder why Princess Zenia is leaving so soon?" asked one of the girls.

She even has a beautiful name, Belissima thought.

"Does she already know which pony she wants?" asked another.

"If Princess Zenia wants to pick Belissima, we should just forget it. She gets whatever she wants," said one of the girls. "I mean, she must. Have you seen all her clothes?"

She gets whatever she wants? Belissima panicked at that news.

"May I please squeeze in here to see this magnificent pony?" another girl said,

pushing through the circle of children to get closer to Belissima. "Even the glitter you make is prettier than anyone else's."

Other children gathered around her, but no one asked about her top grades or her work as lead pony for Earth barn. All their questions were about her looks: Could she turn different colors? Was her mane longer than all the other ponies? Why were her hooves so much sparklier?

Belissima tried her very best to answer their questions politely, but anger was building inside her. She'd never felt something like this before and she didn't know what to do.

When the ceremony was over, Belissima searched the departing crowds and found her mother.

"You looked beautiful out there," her mother said, nudging her with her nose.

Belissima rolled her eyes. "That's all anyone sees in me."

"We must be grateful for the gifts we are given," her mother said softly.

"I know. I've just worked very hard to become good at other things, too, and no one seems to notice."

"Just be yourself, and those wonderful things about you will shine through. And then you will find the right child," her mother said.

Belissima bobbed her head. "I will." But she knew her mother didn't understand. Belissima had big dreams that would never come true as a pageantry horse. *I must be grateful for my gifts*, she reminded herself.

After nudging her mother good-bye, Belissima clomped back to her stall to prepare for the grand ball, that evening's party for the royal families and graduating ponies.

The ball was only going to make things worse, Belissima realized. She'd have to be dressed in her very best accessories. She tried to cheer herself up by remembering all the wonderful foods that would be there, but it didn't help. She wasn't in the mood to go to another event where people would just fuss over her looks while she smiled and nodded.

She had made elaborate plans for the evening. Sunny, a talented first-year pony, was coming over to style her mane and tail. The cape that Belissima had planned to wear hung over the side of her stall. It was a magnificent purple silk that complemented her coat, trimmed in rhinestones. It would attract plenty of attention.

But now she didn't want to do any primping. What would happen if she didn't wear the cape? What if she just showed up with her Earth barn headdress and her mane and tail simply brushed out?

If she wanted people to see her for more than her looks, it didn't make sense to wear something so flashy. And why style her mane in a special design? Her mother had said to be herself. And so she was going to do just that.

She levitated her Ever Ink quill and a piece of paper and wrote a message for

Sunny. "Thanks so very much for the offer, but I don't need you to come over and prepare my mane after all." Then she stomped her hooves to charge up her magic and created a spell to chant. "To Sunny, send this note, so she can see what I wrote!"

The note folded itself and flew through the air, right out the door. Belissima left her stall, hoping the ball would go better than the introduction ceremony.

As Belissima approached the great hall, she spotted an elaborate carriage arriving at the gates. The headmaster had enchanted the rainbow that led to the school so carriages could travel up and over the colorful arch to the hidden academy.

She ducked behind the hedge so she could watch without gawking. The door opened and a coachman rolled out a pink velvet carpet. An elegant older couple both wearing crowns stepped out and headed for the party.

Then Princess Zenia emerged from the
carriage in a poufy pink gown that matched
the velvet rug! It was the same exact shade.
The train of her dress dragged along the
ground until two birds flew out of a box on
top of the carriage, and each picked up part

of the train with their beaks, lifting it off the carpet.

Princess Zenia didn't even seem to notice. She marched into the ballroom with her nose in the air.

Belissima wondered if she'd be holding up her dress like that in a few months. She peered at the dusky sky to find a star to wish upon. *Please don't pick me!*

After a few moments, she went inside the great hall to join the ball—and stay far away from Princess Zenia. That wouldn't be hard. The place was packed with people and ponies dressed in their very finest. Food and drinks covered the tables, and golden troughs overflowed with apple tarts and carrot cake. Hopefully, everyone would be too busy checking out the amazing scene to pay her any attention.

But everyone turned to stare at her. Then whispers started. "She's so beautiful, she doesn't need any fancy gear!"

"Won't she look incredible in a royal portrait!"

Belissima cringed at the thought of standing still for hours so that her painting could be done.

"Smart choice not covering up that beautiful coat with any adornments."

Belissima sighed.

A woman near her gasped. "Why, even her breath is beautiful! She smells like flowers."

Darn. The posy pie was still working!

Belissima stomped over to the dessert table. Her friends Alia and Rasha hurried over.

"Why didn't you get dressed up?" Rasha asked. She wore a beautiful sparkling headdress.

Belissima flicked her tail. "I didn't feel like it. But you two look very lovely. Are you having a nice time?"

Rasha nodded. "Yes, the food is wonderful."

"I've met so many nice children. I can't wait to see who chooses me," Alia said.

Then Belissima noticed Princess Zenia watching her from across the room. "I've got to go," she said, so the girl couldn't talk to her.

But before she could leave, an older woman wearing a crown approached her and stroked her mane. "So wonderful and silky."

How dare the woman march over and touch her without asking. Belissima flicked her tail angrily—and ended up swatting the woman's backside!

Belissima held her breath, waiting for the woman to get angry. But the woman just laughed delightedly.

"Oh, the exquisite thing doesn't even realize how long her lovely tail is!"

Belissima gritted her teeth. What did she have to do to get people to stop commenting on her looks?

Princess Zenia stared at them, her eyes wide and her mouth rounded in a tiny O. Maybe Belissima didn't seem like such a good choice anymore after swatting one of the royal mothers.

Belissima paused as a bold idea bloomed in her mind. It was totally unlike anything she ever would have done before, but she was desperate. She trotted out of the room with a smile. She had big plans for the pageantry exhibition the next day.

CHAPTER 4

Belissima lined up along the exhibition field with the other ponies who had focused on pageantry during their time at the academy. Some of the royal children and their families had spread blankets on the ground and snacked from picnic baskets.

Princess Zenia sat under the shade of a glorious golden tent while two giant white birds flapped their wings, cooling her.

Oh no, thought Belissima. *Maybe it will be*

worse than being a pony who poses and preens. Maybe I'm going to be one of her servants! Luckily, she had a plan that was bound to make the princess think twice about choosing her.

"Ladies and gentlemen, welcome to our exhibition featuring the ponies from the pageantry study group!" Headmistress Valincia's voice rang out over the field. "Today you will see the glorious routines they've created that will shine during any parade or party."

Belissima was the first pony called to perform. She was proud of her routine, and wasn't nervous at all when she trotted onto the field.

And once again, she was appearing

without any special outfit. The sparkly costume she had prepared hung in her stall. The new plan she'd concocted wouldn't work if she were covered with material.

Her music started playing and she began her performance. She cantered to the beat, then ran in a few figure-eight motions. Glitter from her hooves billowed around her. She pranced sideways and held her tail high.

Her routine was going perfectly and she was proud of her hard work. Especially her final move, the capriole.

Most ponies couldn't do it. It was a very advanced move. She leaped into the air, tucked in her front legs and kicked out her back legs at the top of the jump. It would be an incredibly dramatic move during a parade or important event. The crowd offered wild applause.

She galloped in a few more intricate patterns, and stirred up an enormous cloud of glitter as her finale. The crowd cheered as she bowed dramatically.

But instead of returning to the sidelines to chat with the children, Belissima dashed to the field that bordered the forest. She ran through thickets of burrs that clung to her coat and mane. She searched for puddles and sloshed through them, sending mud flying. Branches tore at her coat, leaving a few scratches. She was covered in dirt and burrs by the time she returned to the performance ring.

She stood in front of the crowd waiting

to get their attention. She expected to hear whispers and gasps. While a few spectators did glance her way, no one looked disgusted that she was filthy.

Princess Zenia was even smiling at her!

Belissima trotted over to Rasha. "Why doesn't anyone notice I'm so dirty?"

Rasha looked confused. "What are you talking about?"

"I just ran through the field and got covered with burrs and mud and scratches."

Rasha shook her head. "It must have all come off, because you look just as nice as usual. You don't have a spot on you. No scratches, either."

Belissima turned her head to inspect her coat. She groaned. It was like she'd never even run through that scrubby field! How in the world was she clean? What had happened to her scratches? Now she'd have to come up with another plan to make Princess Zenia think she was the wrong pony to pick.

Belissima tossed and turned all night, worrying and creating her next scheme. What she finally decided on was so bold, it made her jittery. But nothing else she'd tried so far was working, and she could *not* be Princess Zenia's pet, or servant, or whatever horrible plan the princess certainly must have in store for her.

The next morning before heading for the graduate parade, Belissima closed the door to her stall. She levitated the pair of scissors up until they floated in front of her nose. She couldn't believe she was going to do this.

Stomping her hooves, she chanted, "With these shiny shears, snip my mane shorter than the ears!"

The scissors zoomed through the air, and she watched as strands of her mane fell to the barn floor around her.

When the scissors finally stopped, the large pile of long pink strands scattered on the ground made Belissima gasp. But maybe now the royal children would focus on her performance and not her appearance.

She looked in the mirror. It wasn't a cute

short cut like some ponies wore. It was
jagged and uneven. No one would call her
beautiful now.

She trotted to the arena where she'd be
promenading in the parade. Prepared for
the stares and snickers, she raised her

head. But as she got closer to the track she felt something long and silky brushing against her neck.

Impossible, she thought. She stopped trotting and conjured a spell. "In front of me here, make a mirror appear!"

She peered into the glass that suddenly hovered at her side and gasped again. Her mane was back, longer and thicker than ever! Was there no way for her to escape her looks, even for an afternoon?

She was so distracted, she stumbled a few times as she pranced in the parade. She ran off without having a chance to visit with the children or to search for her mother.

Back in her stall, Belissima cut her mane off again. It quickly grew back. She dashed outside, rolled in the dirt, and then hurried back to look in her stall mirror. The dirt simply disappeared. Maybe her Glitter Gift was more than just turning her coat from purple to pink. Maybe her Glitter Gift was always being beautiful!

She sat on the floor, depressed. Perhaps it was her fate to be nothing more than pretty. Which was perfectly fine for a pony who actually loved pageantry. But to her, it seemed utterly useless compared to the skills and Glitter Gifts her friends in the healing group had. Her mother had told her to be grateful for her gifts. Why couldn't she have been blessed with a wonderful healing gift, too?

CHAPTER 5

That afternoon, Belissima went to the flying fields to see her friends in the healing group perform their magical cures. One pony brought dead flowers in a vase back to life. Another healed a baby bird's broken wing. Lavender made a circle of flowers sprout and bloom.

Belissima felt so jealous watching them do such wonderful, helpful things.

Princess Zenia was there, but she wasn't even watching. She was looking at her nails. While most of the other princesses wore simple dresses, Princess Zenia wore another elaborate gown. Her hair was styled into an intricate bun on top of her head.

Belissima imagined the crazy creations the princess would probably make with her mane. She shuddered just thinking of it.

She scanned the crowd, noticing how many ponies and children seemed to be getting along well. On the sidelines, Alia chatted with a princess. She'd seen the two of them together before. They both looked quite happy.

Not far from them, a boy held a carrot for Andover, who munched and crunched as they watched the demonstrations.

Rasha was talking with a girl and waved to Belissima, so she trotted over to them.

"Isn't this so much fun?" Rasha asked. "Have you met any children you really like?"

Belissima sighed. She'd been so worried about Princess Zenia, she hadn't spent much time getting to know the other children.

"No, I haven't. Actually, I haven't talked with too many children."

The princess with Rasha bit her bottom lip. "I should tell you something."

"What is it?" Belissima asked.

"None of the other children are going to pick you at the ceremony."

Tears pricked Belissima's eyes. Did they think she was too naughty after running through the fields? "Why?"

"Because we heard Princess Zenia wants to choose you. And if anyone picks you instead, she will be so angry. Everyone knows you don't want to make Princess Zenia angry. At least that's what I've heard."

Belissima forced a smile and said thanks, then galloped toward her stable. What was she going to do? Princess Zenia was clearly not her perfect match. Should she drop out of the selection ceremony so she couldn't choose her?

Belissima shook her head. She wasn't a quitter. There had to be something else she could do. She was top pony in her class! She could find a solution.

She slowed her trot to a walk and thought about it for a moment. Should she turn to her friends for help?

While she had wonderful friends, she didn't think any of them could understand what she was going through. Any one of them would probably love to be called the prettiest pony to ever have walked through the halls of the academy—and being chosen by Princess Zenia would be a dream come true for any of the ponies in the pageantry group. It sounded very ungrateful to complain about her looks and the fact that she had a princess who wanted her. This was a problem she'd have to work out by herself.

There must be something I haven't thought of yet!

And then the idea hit her. There was one last thing she could try, and what she needed was hidden in the library. She hurried to the big, quiet room in the school.

The library was empty except for the librarian, who looked up and said, "Hello, dear, don't you look lovely as always. Can I help you?"

"Thank you, but I know what I'm looking for."

She headed for the section on the hundred kingdoms and searched for the biggest

book on the shelves: *The Complete History of the Hundred Kingdoms*. With a spell, she levitated the book off the shelf—and gasped. The cookbook wasn't there!

She looked behind other books nearby, but there was no sign of the magic cookbook. She hurried over to the checkout desk.

"Excuse me, can you tell me if the *Magic Treats and Eats Cookbook* is checked out?"

"Certainly!" The pages in the librarian's checkout book turned themselves, until she found what she was looking for. "Ah ha, here it is. That book was checked out yesterday by Stone, in Earth barn."

Belissima nearly shrieked. He was the very last pony who should have that book.

"Thank you!" she called, as she ran out of the library.

CHAPTER 6

Belissima searched Earth barn, but Stone wasn't there. She trotted along the training field and went to the banquet hall, but there was no sign of him.

Where could he be? Then she smelled a delicious scent wafting from the kitchen.

"Oh no."

Quietly, she entered the kitchen. Stone was reading the cookbook, and the counter was covered with ingredients.

"What are you doing?" she asked.

He looked up, surprised. "I'm making a recipe."

"From the magic cookbook. Stone, no pranks during selection week. It's already too stressful. Jokes are not appropriate right now."

He flared his nostrils. "What makes you think I'm making a prank recipe? There are nice, helpful ones in here, too."

"You like to play jokes. All the time. And you told the first-years in Earth barn you wanted to make *atchoo* pie." She tapped her hoof angrily.

"I was kidding about that." He sighed. "I wasn't planning to pull a prank. Honest. I wish everyone didn't think I'm

nothing but a joker. I'm more than that, you know."

Belissima didn't know what to say.

"Do you know what it's like when everyone thinks all you're interested in is goofing around? Making jokes? I like to have fun, but that's not the only thing about me. I thought if I could make this one special recipe I had in mind, the ponies might see me differently. You don't know how bad I feel sometimes."

Belissima lowered her voice. "Yes, I do, actually. And I'm sorry. I know exactly what it's like for everyone to see you only one way. Of course you're more than just a jokester, Stone."

Stone looked down and softened his voice. "Thanks, Belissima. That means a lot coming from you. You work so hard in your classes, and you're so nice to all the ponies in school."

She was touched that he said nothing about her looks. "You're very welcome. So tell me, if you're not making a prank cake, what are you making?"

Stone smiled. "This might sound crazy, but I think I might be able to shoot a rainbow from my horn."

"What? You're not teasing me?" she asked.

He shook his head. "I told you, this isn't a joke. I can shoot sparks, and I think if I combine a few of these recipes, I could make a rainbow. Just for a short time."

Belissima paused. She didn't want to discourage him and tell him that would be impossible, especially for a first-year student, but she also didn't want him to be disappointed when he discovered it was too hard of a spell for him. "Stone, that sounds amazing, but that would require incredibly strong magic."

He flattened his ears. "You don't think I could do it?"

"That's not what I'm saying. Of course you should try. I just want you to be aware of the difficulty in what you're trying to do. But why now? It's a busy, fun week. The first-years don't have classes. Why spend all this time in the kitchen trying to master an extremely difficult recipe?"

Stone tilted his head and thought for a moment. "I've got all this extra time on my hands, and I don't want to get in trouble. So I just thought, wouldn't it be nice to see a rainbow during the selection ceremony? It would enhance everyone's magic. It would make the day even more special, don't you think?" He sounded quite sincere.

"It certainly would. I'd love to see a rainbow. I hope you can make it happen. Can I take a look at the cookbook for a moment?"

"Sure, I'm still mixing up my latest batch. So far, I was able to shoot mist from my horn and then I also made it sound like a trumpet."

Belissima giggled. "That's a good start."

"I'm sure I'll have a lot of fun with those discoveries someday. I may not be one-hundred-percent prankster, but I do like my jokes!" He grinned, showing all his teeth.

Belissima couldn't help but laugh. "You

know what? We all enjoy your jokes, too, Stone. You're a lot of fun."

Stone whinnied and got back to work on his recipe.

She paged through the cookbook and found the recipe she was looking for. A few of the ingredients would be tough to find, but it didn't seem too hard. "Stone, can you

leave the cookbook in the kitchen? I'd like to try something tomorrow."

"Of course! But you better not pull a prank," he said, laughing. "I'm kidding, I know you'd never do that."

Don't be so sure, she thought.

CHAPTER 7

Belissima was up before the sun, collecting dewdrops from a forest fern and dropping them in a glass bottle. There were quite a few odd ingredients she needed to find. The sour mushroom was the hardest to locate. It looked very much like the swamp mushroom, which was quite poisonous, so she had to be sure she'd found the right one. Finally, she found the tiny green mushroom growing under a log. It did not have orange spots on its underside like the swamp mush-room, so she knew it was safe.

She added two mushrooms to a bag looped around her neck. The recipe seemed much more advanced than the posy pie and cloud candy the other ponies had made. She hoped it would work.

While everyone else gathered to watch the demonstrations by the ponies in the guardianship group, Belissima snuck into the kitchen. She felt bad missing her friends' performances, but at least she wouldn't run into Princess Zenia.

The recipe took hours to make. But that wasn't surprising considering the magic it would cast. She levitated the cake back to her stall right before the ponies' nine o'clock curfew. Since she didn't know how long the spell would last, she decided she would sneak a piece to the selection ceremony the next day and take a bite right before the ceremony.

The next morning, Belissima was the last pony to arrive at the arena. A piece of the

cake was tucked in a small bag she had brought with her. She still couldn't believe what she was about to do. It pretty much guaranteed she wouldn't be chosen today.

"Where have you been? It's almost time to start," Alia said.

"I overslept," Belissima said.

But that wasn't true. She had been working up her courage to come to the selection ceremony and carry through her plan. She had no idea if it was going to work, but it was time to try. She nudged open the bag and quickly ate a bite of the cake. The pleasant cinnamony taste surprised her. She'd been expecting a prank cake to taste horrible. *I hope I made it right!* Maybe she'd spent all that time baking for nothing!

"I'm so nervous," Rasha said. "I hope Princess Palina picks me, I really liked her."

"I'm sure she will, Rasha." Belissima forced a smile, wishing she felt as hopeful for her own future right now.

The headmaster addressed the crowd. "Royal families of the hundred kingdoms, welcome to the Spring Selection Day Ceremony. Today, the royal children who have completed their leadership classes are invited to choose their perfect pony match to help rule their land."

Belissima lifted her hoof to see if the magic recipe had taken effect yet, but she saw nothing different about her leg. She gulped nervously. Maybe she hadn't made the recipe correctly.

"The names of the children in today's ceremony were drawn in a lottery to determine who should go first," the headmaster said. "And you will see those names revealed now on the tally board behind me."

Everyone turned to look at the board as the names appeared. Chatter filled the arena. Princess Zenia was first!

"Please let the magic cake work, please let it work," Belissima whispered to herself.

Just then, a rainbow arched over the arena, and the colorful light enveloped her. She was standing in the very end of it! Everyone pointed at the rainbow in the sky, shouting and cheering. Belissima scanned the crowd and sure enough, Stone stood off to the side alone, shooting the rainbow from his horn.

He did it! I can't believe it!

"What good luck!" said Ranger. "Our magic will be even stronger as we perform our last routine!"

"Wow!" Rasha said. "Yours is going to be extra powerful, Belissima, since you were standing right in it!"

Belissima gulped. "I hope so."

The ponies whinnied and cheered.

"Look, it's Stone!" someone hollered.

"Stone's making the rainbow!" Rasha said.

"Thanks, Stone," Alia cried.

The rainbow quickly faded, but Belissima still couldn't believe he had found a way to cast the spell. She was so impressed.

The excited whispering in the arena quickly turned to gasps then shrieks and even some laughter. People were pointing at her. Belissima turned her head to inspect her coat. Sure enough, her soft purple coat was covered in moldy green spots. The cake had worked. Better than she had imagined, even. The moldy spots were bigger and fuzzier than she'd expected. They were a darker green, too. The rainbow must have really enhanced the power of the recipe.

"She looks like a mushroom!" someone hollered.

The pointing and laughing continued.

Belissima was surprised by how much it hurt her heart. She wasn't used to being made fun of. She'd only ever had people and ponies fuss over her. But this was what she wanted.

"What happened?" Rasha asked her. "Let me cover you with my cape."

Belissima held her head high. "No, I'm fine. I'm glad this happened. Now someone will have to choose me for the right reasons."

She wasn't sure if that would really happen, though. And she didn't know how long the spots would last.

But even if they quickly faded away, Princess Zenia might worry they'd come back. No way would she choose Belissima now. Belissima felt bad playing such a rotten trick, but it was the only way she could be sure she didn't end up with the totally wrong child.

"I ask that you all please settle down so we may begin the ceremony," Headmistress Valincia announced. "Princess Zenia, you were picked first in our lottery. Please approach the ponies and make your selection."

Slowly, the perfect princess rose from her throne and walked toward the ponies. Her gaze swept across the group, and Belissima was relieved her coat was still covered in spots. A princess that refined could never choose her as a pet. The truth was, probably no one would choose Belissima today. Her mother would be so disappointed.

If she weren't chosen, Belissima would spend another six months at the school until the next selection week in the fall. Maybe she could take extra healing classes. It wouldn't be horrible.

But Princess Zenia walked right over to Belissima. She tilted her head and stared at her.

Belissima was panicked. "Look at me. Look at these horrible spots!" she said. "You don't want to pick me."

One corner of Zenia's mouth curled up. "I most certainly do." She turned to the head-master. "I choose Belissima as my royal pet. I am certain we will be a perfect match."

Belissima froze. Was this just a bad dream?

CHAPTER 8

The crowd cheered and the headmaster said, "Congratulations to you both, and to you especially, Belissima, for being the First Pony chosen this ceremony."

That meant her picture would be added to the display in the great hall. She wondered if it would show her ugly spots.

"We'll see you tomorrow for the good-bye ceremony," the headmistress said. "Best wishes for a happy future together."

Belissima fought to hold back her tears as she left the stage and followed the princess out of the arena.

Princess Zenia spun in place and clasped her hands together. "I can't wait to show you your new home. My father, the king, had a stall made especially for my Glitter Pony on the ship we'll take to sail to our land. And wait until you see your stable! It's gorgeous. I just know we're a perfect match for each other."

Belissima forced a smile and nodded. She thought about telling the princess they were anything but a perfect match. That they'd never be happy together, that she should go choose a different pony. But it was too late for that. She was going to have to make the best of this situation. "Don't worry about my spots. They should fade away soon."

"Does this happen to you often?" the princess asked.

"No, I made a recipe from a magic cookbook. But since a rainbow appeared right as I ate it, it intensified the spell. Rainbows strengthen Glitter Pony magic."

Princess Zenia's eyes widened. "A magic cookbook? Can I see it?"

"Sure, maybe there's a reversal spell in it." Belissima led her to the kitchen where she'd left the book the night before.

"Most of them are pleasant tricks but a few are pranks. Like the one I made. They're supposed to be temporary." She didn't want to explain why she'd given herself spots and she was glad the princess didn't ask.

"What is the name of the one that gave you the spots?"

"Spotty Mushroom Surprise."

Princess Zenia flipped through the book until she found it. She scrunched her eyebrows together as she read the ingredients. "What is a sour mushroom?"

"That's a rare mushroom found in the forest. The same color as my spots. Very hard to find."

Princess Zenia turned a few more pages. "I don't see a reversal recipe. Are there any recipes that could turn my hair a different color, the way your coat turns?"

Right, so we can just change hair and coat

colors all day long. Belissima frowned. "I haven't looked through the whole book. But I'm not sure how these recipes work on a human. They're meant for Glitter Ponies."

"Still, they might be fun to try." Princess Zenia pulled out a small notebook from the pocket of her dress and jotted down a few notes.

"What else should I see on campus? Since we're leaving tomorrow night, are there any places you'd like to visit one last time before we go home?" the princess asked.

Home. The word stunned Belissima for a moment. She'd be leaving for a new home after spending two years at the academy. She'd be leaving behind her friends, her teachers, her classes. There were so many things she was going to miss here. "Why don't I show you some of the most special places in the academy?"

"That sounds wonderful."

"Let's go to the stables to get my saddle and we can ride," Belissima said. *So I can appreciate this beautiful school one last time before heading to my sad new home.*

CHAPTER 9

After saddling up, Belissima took the princess on a tour of the school grounds. She showed her Earth barn and the banquet hall and all the wonderful places on campus.

"There's one more special place to visit. But it will take a while to get there."

"Let's go!"

Belissima ran toward the trail in the woods that led to the river with the seaponies.

Princess Zenia squealed with delight as they galloped through the forest.

They got to the river, and Belissima sang a quick song. Seaponies always rose to the surface when they heard nice music.

Soon, Marina's head popped up from under water. A few of her friends were with her.

"Hi, Marina! I wanted to say good-bye before I leave school. This is Princess Zenia."

"Your perfect match?" Marina asked.

Belissima forced a smile. "She picked me during the selection ceremony."

"It is very nice to meet you, Princess Zenia," Marina said softly. Seaponies were very shy with creatures above the water.

"You too! I never swam with seaponies before. Mind if I join you?" the princess asked.

"That would be quite nice. I never swam with a human princess!" Marina said.

Belissima's mouth hung open. This perfect princess was going to get wet? "You're going to ruin your dress!"

"Don't worry. I've got hundreds of other dresses."

Of course you do, Belissima thought to herself, remembering who she was talking to.

Princess Zenia climbed off Belissima's back, lifted the skirt of her dress, and ran toward the river. A big splash soaked Belissima when the princess did a cannonball into the river.

Belissima's mouth hung open.

When Princess Zenia came up, she held two handfuls of seaweed. She plopped one on top of her head and placed bits on her face. "Now I look like you!"

Belissima laughed. Maybe the princess wouldn't be totally horrible to live with.

The princess waved for her to come in the water. "Join me! It's lots of fun!" The seaponies raced circles around the princess and she giggled.

Belissima waded into the water near the princess. Would that remove her spots? "Is the green mold gone?"

"No," said Princess Zenia.

Belissima was embarrassed to admit it, but the spots were really starting to bother her.

"Cheer up," said the princess. "Maybe we can decorate them with flowers and no one will notice the spots!" She snapped her fingers. "Or my seamstress could make you a lovely cape to cover them up."

"Yes, perhaps." Belissima sighed. The endless hours of playing dress-up would soon begin.

After swimming for a while, Belissima walked onto the riverbank. "We should get back for dinner."

"Oh, that's right. I need to change and fix my hair!" Princess Zenia said as she sloshed out of the water. "Do you know any spells that could dry and style my hair quickly?"

Belissima gritted her teeth. "I don't know. And I'm afraid to try. I might mess it up."

"That's all right. Hopefully, it'll dry on the way back. Oh, I almost forgot! I had matching capes made for us. I'll drop yours off after I get ready."

"Okay," Belissima said quietly. *Guess I better get used to this.*

The princess climbed onto the saddle and Belissima trotted back to school, holding back her tears. She looked horrible, the princess had big plans for dressing her up, and soon she'd be leaving this lovely school forever.

Belissima dropped the princess near her carriage, and she headed toward Earth barn. She really wanted to talk to her mother about everything troubling her.

Belissima saw her mother standing in front of her barn and she charged toward her. "Mom!"

Her mother galloped to meet her and nudged her nose.

"Oh, it all went so wrong, Mom!"

"You were First Pony. That was a wonderful thing."

"But I'm covered in spots. They won't go away!" Belissima explained how she'd made the magic recipe and how the rainbow intensified the magic. "I thought the princess wouldn't pick me if I looked like that."

"Maybe she could see beyond the spots."

"No, I don't think that's it. She made up her mind that we were a perfect match because of the way I look. She's so pretty and she just wants a pretty pony to show off and dress up." Belissima sighed. "We're not a perfect match. I wish she hadn't picked me."

Belissima heard a gasp behind her.

"That's really what you think?" Princess Zenia sniffed. "I can't believe this! After everything I saw this week, I thought we were meant to be together." She dropped the silky pink cape she'd been holding and ran off.

"Wait!" Belissima called, but the princess kept running.

"Give her time to cool off," her mother said. "Then you can talk. You'll find some things in common. Give her a chance."

Belissima's heart ached. While she wasn't thrilled about being Princess Zenia's match, she hadn't wanted to hurt her.

Belissima levitated the cape off the ground and shook off the dirt. She swapped her saddle for the silky garment and headed for the great hall. Maybe the princess would forgive her when she saw her dressed up.

CHAPTER 10

Belissima scanned the great hall for the princess, but she didn't see her. When she spotted Zenia's parents she trotted up to them. "Where is the princess?"

"We thought she was with you," the queen said.

The king sighed. "She must be off on another one of her adventures."

"Adventures?" Belissima asked, surprised.

"Yes, that daughter of mine is a wild child. She hates getting dressed up and performing her royal duties. She promised to be on her very best behavior while she was here. I thought by choosing such a well-groomed, beautiful pony like you, she was finally settling down, making a good choice," the queen said.

"The princess doesn't like getting dressed up?" Belissima asked, shocked.

The king laughed. "The queen has had hundreds of gowns made for her, hoping that she might become interested in something other than tromping through the woods and catching frogs."

"I figured she was trying to find herself a

prince, but no. She was trying to find the best jumper in the land." The queen rolled her eyes.

"Princess Zenia likes to explore?" Belissima asked.

"That's probably what she's doing now. Do you have any idea where she might be?" the king asked.

Belissima looked down, feeling horrible. She'd been complaining about no one seeing beyond her appearances, and she'd done the very same thing to Princess Zenia! "I'm afraid I upset her." Belissima explained what had happened. "I don't know where she went. She was dressed for dinner; I thought she'd come here."

"I'll send my guards to look for her," the king said.

"I'll check the river. We visited there earlier today." Belissima tossed off her cape, raced out of the great hall, and galloped across the fields to the forest. "Princess Zenia?" she cried. "Princess Zenia!"

There was no sign of her when she got to the river. "Marina! Please rise!" She was too upset to sing.

Marina quickly came to the surface. "What's wrong? Where's your princess?"

"I don't know. She's missing. Did she come back here?"

Marina shook her head. "No, I haven't seen her."

"Thanks, Marina." Belissima raced back to school, uncertain what to do. She searched all the places they'd visited on campus, but there was no sign of her.

As the sun set, Belissima stood outside Earth barn. Big tears trailed down her cheeks. This was all her fault.

A silvery orb popped open next to her. "Belissima!" It was Headmaster Elegius, the only teacher on campus who could teleport. "You're needed in the healing center. Princess Zenia is very sick. Go at once!"

CHAPTER 11

Belissima arrived in the healing center breathless. "What happened?"

"One of our guards found her injured in the forest," the queen said. "She had a bag with her like she was collecting things."

"She was collapsed in a small ravine," the guard said, holding a cloth over a cut on his arm. "But she hasn't woken since I found her."

"Do you have any idea what she was doing?" the king asked.

"None at all," Belissima said.

"I'm afraid I'm not familiar with human ailments," said Phina, the academy healer. "If she were a pony, I'd have all kind of potions to try."

"Let me see her bag, please," Belissima said.

The queen handed the small silk satchel to Belissima. She dumped it out on a nearby table. There was a fern leaf and moss. A shiny rock sparkled on the table. And then she spotted a familiar green mushroom. The same color as the spots on her coat.

"These are some of the ingredients in the magic recipe that left these green spots on my coat," Belissima explained. "But why would she be collecting them?"

Belissima walked over to the princess, who lay limp on top of a table. "Hi, princess," she said softly. "We're all terribly worried about you. I'm very sorry you heard those awful things I said. I didn't mean them. And I know the truth. Your mother explained everything. I'm so sorry I judged you without knowing you. You have to tell me what happened. How did you get hurt?"

The princess's eyes slowly opened. "Belissima," she whispered, sitting up. "I was trying ... to show ..." She coughed, and the queen rushed over with a glass of water.

Princess Zenia took a few sips and lay back down. "I thought if I had green spots, too ... you'd know ... I don't care how you look. Or how I look. I picked you ... because you seemed like fun. All those funny tricks you played."

A huge lump formed in Belissima's throat. "Princess, that was so kind of you to consider becoming spotty, too. But I don't

understand what happened. Why are you sick?"

"I didn't have . . ." She reached for Belissima, her hands covered in cuts. "I didn't have time to make the recipe, so I thought if I ate the ingredients it might work."

Phina looked over the ingredients spread out on the table. "But none of these should have made you sick, deary."

Princess Zenia opened her mouth but no words came out. Her eyes closed and her breaths were shallow. She fell back onto the table.

The king and queen hurried to her side.

What should I do? Belissima tried to remember all the lessons from her healing classes, but they'd never dealt with anything like this.

"Wait a minute," Belissima said. She returned to the table of items the princess had collected and took another look at the mushroom. "That's not a sour mushroom.

It's a swamp mushroom. Look, it has a few orange spots on the underside. I didn't notice them before."

"But those are poisonous!" Phina said.

"What's the cure?" the king demanded.

"There is no cure," Phina said quietly.

Belissima went back to Zenia, stomping her hooves on the ground. She may not have been in the healing study group, but she had taken a few introductory classes, like all the ponies at the academy. There had to be something she could do.

"This sick girl needs a cure, find the perfect one for sure." She chanted the rhyme again and again.

"It's not working," the queen cried.

She tried another spell. "Make this girl heal, bring back her health and zeal."

The princess didn't stir.

"Oh, this is awful. Just awful," Phina said.

"Get the headmaster and headmistress," Belissima shouted. "There must be something they can do."

Phina hurried out of the room as Belissima's mom entered the great hall. "Are you okay?"

"No," Belissima said, her voice thick. "I didn't listen to you. I wasn't thankful for my gifts. I ruined everything."

"Honey, it's not your fault," her mother said, but Belissima didn't believe her.

Headmaster Elegius and Headmistress

Valinica charged in and went over to the girl.

"Is she going to die?" the king asked through his tears.

"Thankfully, the swamp mushroom isn't deadly," Headmaster Elegius said, "but it can leave its victims in a permanent sleep."

CHAPTER 12

The queen fell into the king's arms, sobbing.

Tears rolled down Belissima's cheeks, too. She walked to the princess and stood over her. "I'm so sorry. I never even gave us a chance to get to know each other. I will never forgive myself." One after another, Belissima's tears dropped onto the princess's cheeks, shining like little gems.

Princess Zenia's eyes fluttered open. She sucked in a deep breath. "Oh. Oh my." She sat up. "I feel so much better. What did you do?"

Belissima couldn't reply for a few moments, she was so surprised. "Nothing. I was just standing here, crying."

Everyone in the room stood there, stunned. "It's a miracle," the queen said.

"No, not a miracle—magic," said the headmaster.

"What do you mean?" asked Belissima. "I didn't do magic. I tried casting healing spells but they didn't work."

"Your tears," the headmaster explained. "I suspect they have healing magic."

Belissima looked at the scratches

covering Zenia's hand. She let a few tears fall on them. They disappeared.

"You have a hidden Glitter Gift," the headmistress said. "You're a healing pony."

"What? Impossible," Belissima said.

"Try healing my wound," the guard said, holding out his arm.

Belissima thought again of how sick Zenia had been, and tears welled in her eyes once more. They splashed onto the guard's arm.

"Nothing's happening," he said. "The gash is still there."

"How odd," the headmaster said, tapping his hoof. "The princess has another scratch on her arm. Try healing that."

Belissima shed a few tears onto the remaining scratch.

"It's gone!" Zenia cried.

"I don't understand," Belissima said.

The headmistress smiled. "It would appear that you have a hidden Glitter Gift. One that is indeed healing—your perfect match. If Princess Zenia hadn't chosen you, you might have never discovered this. Have there been any other instances of you healing?"

Belissima thought about her own scratches, the ones that disappeared after she ran through the fields. She remembered how her mane grew back. "Actually, yes. Now that I think about it, I've healed myself without even trying."

"So you can heal yourself and your perfect match," the headmistress said. "What a wonderful gift."

The princess grinned. "I knew you were my perfect match."

She threw her arms around Belissima's neck.

Then she gasped. "Your spots disappeared when I hugged you!"

"Thank goodness," Belissima said. "I'm never going to take my pretty purple coat for granted again."

Belissima's mother came over to her. "Now you have another gift to be grateful for. I'm so proud of you and how hard you've worked these past two years. And I'm so glad you found such a wonderful, perfect match."

"Thanks, Mom. I'll miss you."

"I'll miss you, too. But I'm excited to hear about your new life. Make sure you tell me about all your adventures together."

Belissima grinned. "I will."

"I can't wait to go home tomorrow," said the princess.

"Neither can I," Belissima said. And she really meant it, even if she had to dress up and prance around every once in a while. As long as she was with Princess Zenia, everything would be fine. They were a perfect match after all.

Welcome to the
ENCHANTED PONY ACADEMY,
where dreams sparkle and magic shines!